It's Your Bed, Fred!

By Janelle Cherrington
Illustrated by Lauren Attinello

Random House
New York

TM & copyright © 1999 by The Jim Henson Company. All rights reserved under International and Pan-American Copyright Conventions. Published in the United States by Random House, Inc., New York, and simultaneously in Canada by Random House of Canada Limited, Toronto.
MUPPET PRESS, MUPPETS, characters, and character likenesses are trademarks of The Jim Henson Company.
Library of Congress Catalog Card Number: 98-66975   ISBN 0-679-89383-0

www.randomhouse.com/kids   www.henson.com

Printed in the United States of America   10 9 8 7 6 5 4 3 2 1

JELLYBEAN BOOKS is a trademark of Random House, Inc.

I don't want to be in bed—
I'll pretend that it's a tent instead.

Or a sailboat in the breeze,
swirling, twirling 'round with ease.

I was wrong. I spoke too soon.
This boat is really a balloon!

Now we're floating way up high...
we're on a spaceship in the sky!

Magic carpets fly high, too—
watch us as we zoom by you!

I see snow and trees ahead.
We're racing downhill on a sled!

Snow is cold and so is ice,
but igloos can be awfully nice!

So can houses built in trees.
I really would like one of these!

Or is this a den for sleeping bears?
Is that Wally over there?

I'm suddenly a sleepyhead!
So now I'm glad my bed's a bed.

When what I really need is rest,
my bed's the place that I love best!